E
PO

Poulet, Virginia

Blue Bug's book of
colors

BLUE BUG'S BOOK of COLORS

By Virginia Poulet

Illustrated by Peggy Perry Anderson

INTRODUCING NAT

CHILDRENS PRESS, CHICAGO

To
Jennifer Leigh
and
James William

Library of Congress Cataloging in Publication Data

Poulet, Virginia.
   Blue bug's book of colors.

   SUMMARY: Blue bug discovers through trial and error
how colors mix to make different colors.
   [1.   Color—Fiction]   I.   Anderson, Peggy Perry.
II.   Title
PZ7.P86Bb   [E]   80-23229
ISBN 0-516-03442-1

      6 7 8 9 10 11 12 R 89 88 87 86

Blue Bug and his friend Nat discovered that...

red and yellow make...

orange,

yellow and blue make...

green,

blue and red make...

13

purple,

red and white make...

17

pink,

red and green make...

brown,

black and white make...

gray,

and everything together
makes...

a mess!

Feebee made them clean up.